MOON SOUP

★

MOON SOUP

Lisa Desimini

Hyperion Books for Children
New York

Printed in Hong Kong.

For information address Hyperion Books for Children,

114 Fifth Avenue, New York, New York 10011.

First Edition

1 3 5 7 9 10 8 6 4 2

Library of Congress Cataloging–in–Publication Data

Desimini, Lisa.

Moon soup / Lisa Desimini.

p. cm.

Summary: Moon soup contains fantastic ingredients, and when it's
ready it must be eaten while sitting on the moon.

ISBN 1-56282-463-5—ISBN 1-56282-464-3 (lib. bdg.)

[1. Soups—Fiction. 2. Moon—Fiction.] I. Title.

PZ7.D4505Mo 1993 [E]—dc20 92-55041 CIP AC

The artwork for each picture is prepared with layers of oil glazing on bristol paper.

This book is set in 28-point ITC Esprit.

Teachers: Matt, Mark, Patti, and Evelyn Leavens

Maureen

Hi! Mom + Dad

Jerry was in L.A. 1992

For Natalie + Brian

Lauri,
Thank you for the inspired thoughts

Charlene
Marlene

Hi Grandma

Giavanna

Hi Valerie!

Toni - thanks for your support and friendship

I've got the house to myself and I'm making moon soup.

It all begins at sunrise,

when the rooster cock-a-doodle-dos

and the hens lay their eggs.

Six eggs are what I need,
no more, no less.

I toss them into the biggest pot I can find.
If not, an umbrella will do.

There is
no milk in
moon soup.

Purple is the main ingredient.

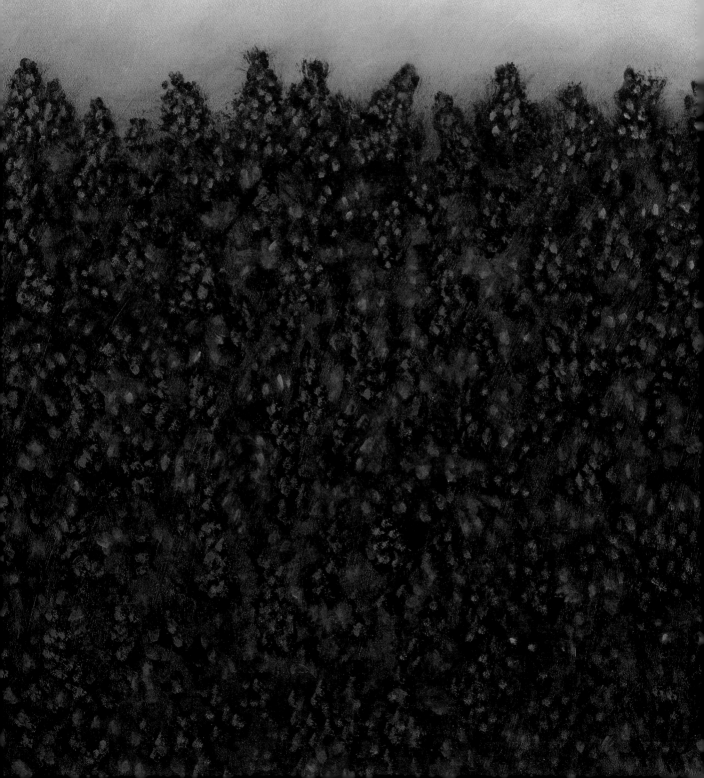

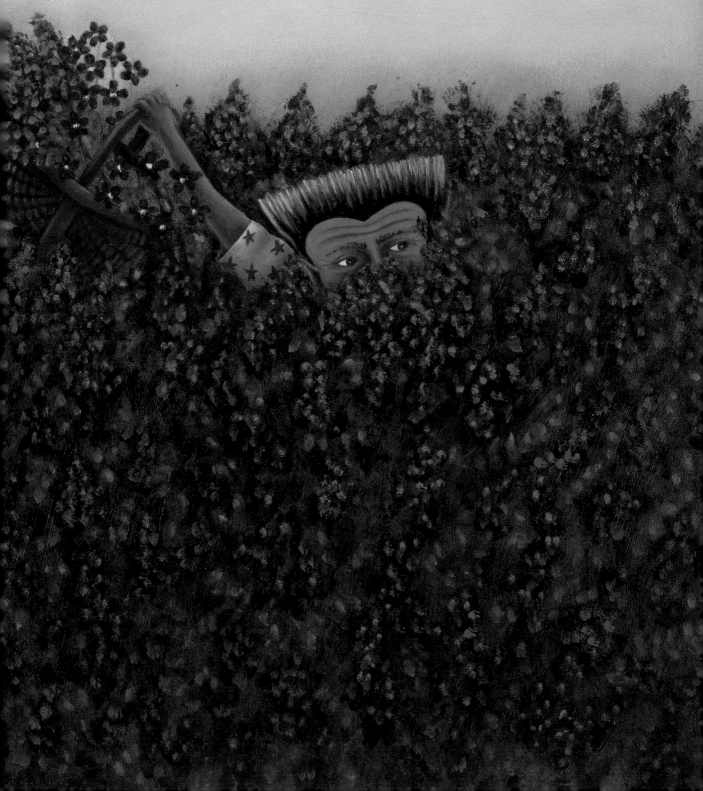

I gather lilacs and violets at noon,

grapes

and

eggplants—

even an emperor's robe.
I mix and blend well.

Party
at
4:00
p.m.

I need teacups galore.
I have a party and invite all my friends.
We drink tea with pie
and eat cookies shaped like stars.

Everyone sings and laughs and talks.

They drop their cups into the soup
on their way out the door.

I stir once or twice.

As the clock strikes six
I grab a giant net
and scoop a peachy sunset.

Then I turn on
some music and
dance, letting the
soup simmer until
the moon is high.

I'm through
gathering
and
adding.

I've mixed,

blended,

tossed,

scooped,
and

stirred.

My wings are in place.

I fly
through
the window
and zoom past
the stars,
because
moon soup
can't
be eaten
in the
kitchen
or the yard, in the meadow
or my room.

Moon soup must be eaten
while sitting on the moon.